THE WHISPER BROOK DETECTIVE AGENCY

RACHAEL CLATTERBUCK

TABLE OF CONTENTS

THE WHISPER BROOK DETECTIVE AGENCY SERIES: CASE 1 CASSEROLE NAPPER

CHAPTER 1:
TROUBLE AT WHISPER BROOK

Whisper Brook Apartments was a quiet place, or at least, it used to be. Tucked between a row of shady palm trees and a sleepy bookstore, the building seemed perfectly normal on the outside. But inside, something was always happening… especially if you were a cat or a dog.

The humans might have missed the signs, but the animals knew the truth: Whisper Brook was a place of secrets.

And today, it was a place of drama.

It all started with a casserole. Not just any casserole, Mrs. Higgins' famous tuna casserole, the one she made every Sunday for herself and sometimes shared with her furry neighbors.

Mrs. Higgins, the sweetest lady in the whole building, was the heart of Whisper Brook. She wore cardigans with cat buttons, fed the birds at precisely 7:15 every morning, and always remembered to scratch behind Priss the corgi's ears when she passed by.

But today, Mrs. Higgins was upset.

"She left the oven door wide open," Priss whispered from her spot by the front window, ears perked. "And she said something about 'vanishing tuna.' This is serious."

"She sounded distraught," added Milkshake. The sleek gray cat lounging dramatically on a sunlit windowsill. "Tragic, really. But also… quite fishy."

"Oh, dear," murmured Alice from her perch on the high bookshelf. Alice was the oldest cat in Whisper Brook and the wisest by far. "If her casserole is truly gone, this could shake the entire apartment's balance. No more Sunday leftovers. No more post-casserole naps. No more… happiness."

Priss stood tall—well, as tall as a corgi could. "Then we have to help. We must find that casserole."

"Speak for yourself," Milkshake said with a yawn, though her ears twitched with interest. "I don't chase missing food."

"You do if it's tuna," Alice said, narrowing her eyes.

Milkshake said nothing.

Just then, a blur of fur and paws scrambled through the door. "Did someone say 'casserole'?!" barked Pretzel, the ever-enthusiastic Australian Shepherd, nearly tripping over his own tail. "I love casserole! Where is it? Can I sniff it? Wait—is it here?!"

"No, Pretzel," Priss sighed. "It's gone. Vanished. Missing without a trace."

Pretzel gasped. "A mystery! I love mysteries! And snacks! And mysterious snacks!"

Alice gracefully jumped down from her perch. "Then it's settled. The humans may be clueless, but we are not. The casserole won't find itself. We must form a team."

"A team?" Milkshake's tail flicked. "Does it come with matching hats?"

"No hats," Priss said firmly. "Just noses, claws, paws, and determination."

"Can I be the one who runs in circles when we get excited?" Pretzel asked hopefully.

"You already are," Priss muttered.

The four animals stood together in the hallway of Whisper Brook Apartments. Behind them, Mrs. Higgins could be heard pacing and muttering about "spices and sabotage."

A new mystery had arrived. And this time, the animals were ready.

The Case of the Missing Casserole had officially begun.

CHAPTER 2:
THE FURRY FOUR

Whisper Brook Apartments wasn't exactly known for its crime-solving teams, but if it had been, these four would've had their own office by now. Instead, they had the hallway outside Unit 3B, and that would have to do.

Priss took the lead, as usual. Her tan and white fur was perfectly groomed, and her little legs moved with purpose. "Okay, team. We need to gather clues, question witnesses, and track scents. This is our mission."

Pretzel bounced beside her like a furry pogo stick. "Mission! Yes! I love missions! Also, can we sniff things? Like everything? Please?"

Milkshake rolled her eyes, but even she couldn't hide her curiosity. "Just don't sniff me, floppy ears. And if I get fur in my whiskers from that rug again, I'm out."

Alice trotted along behind them at her own pace. Her long black fur was flecked with silver, like a shadow touched by moonlight. She had lived in Whisperbrook since it had carpet in the hallways and a cranky landlord named Stan. She knew things. Things the others didn't.

"The last time anything went missing around here," Alice said thoughtfully, "it was the mystery of the disappearing dryer sheets. Turned out to be a squirrel with a static problem. But this… this feels different."

"Tuna is way more important than dryer sheets," Pretzel said, sniffing the floor and the wall and then accidentally licking a dust bunny. "Blegh. Nope. That was not tuna."

Priss ignored him. "Let's go over what we know. Mrs. Higgins made the casserole last night. She left it on the windowsill to cool, then went to watch her favorite mystery show. When she came back, it was gone."

"Gone," Milkshake echoed dramatically. "Stolen. Swiped. Snatched."

Alice's whiskers twitched. "Or simply… eaten."

There was a stunned silence.

"You don't think she ate it herself?" Priss asked.

"She might've," Alice said. "Or maybe someone else did. The question is—who?"

"Do we have suspects?" Pretzel asked, standing on his hind legs like a meerkat. He promptly knocked over a potted plant. "Oops. That wasn't a clue. That was dirt."

"We'll start with the scene of the crime," Priss decided. "Back to Mrs. Higgins' apartment. With our noses, our brains, and our overly dramatic commentary—"

"Hey," Milkshake interrupted. "That's my thing."

"—we'll crack this case wide open."

Together, the furry four turned toward Apartment 3B. The hallway stretched ahead like a runway, the beige carpet lit by the sun pouring through the high windows. Somewhere inside, Mrs. Higgins was still fussing over her lost casserole.

And just maybe, a clue was waiting to be discovered.

CHAPTER 3:
SCENE OF THE CRIME

Apartment 3B smelled like lemongrass, cat treats, and just the faintest trace of... heartbreak.

Mrs. Higgins sat on her floral loveseat, clutching an empty casserole dish. Her beloved calico, Pudding, curled on her lap with her paws tucked under, blissfully unaware of the crisis at hand. A cooling rack sat on the windowsill, tragically empty.

"She just keeps muttering about a crime against cuisine," whispered Priss, peeking from beneath the kitchen table. "We have to be careful. She's fragile."

"She's dramatic," Milkshake corrected. "There's a difference."

Pretzel, meanwhile, was busy sniffing every corner of the kitchen. His nose bumped the trash can, the fridge, and even the bottom of Mrs. Higgins' fuzzy slippers.

"Focus, Pretzel," Priss reminded him. "Look for clues."

"I am!" he said, sniffing deeply near the floor. "Something smells fishy."

"That's because it was fishy," Milkshake said dryly. "It was a tuna casserole."

"No," Pretzel said, ears twitching. "I mean, it smells like... leftovers. Like a trail!"

He bounded toward the hallway, nose to the carpet.

"Wait," Alice said softly. She padded to the windowsill and raised one paw. "There's something here."

The other animals gathered around. Alice delicately nudged a few crumbs into view with her paw.

"Casserole crumbs," she confirmed. "Definitely tuna. And something else…"

"Cheese," Milkshake said after a sniff. "Sharp cheddar. Quality stuff. I respect that."

Priss's tail wagged. "That means the culprit didn't eat it all in one place. They took it somewhere. Maybe dropped bits along the way."

Alice peered closer. "Look here—fur. Not Mrs. Higgins', not ours. Light gray, short… unfamiliar."

"A stranger?" Priss asked.

"Maybe," Alice said. "Or a neighbor with secrets."

At that moment, Pretzel came racing back in, skidding on the hardwood floor. "Guys! You have to see this! There's a trail! It goes under the laundry room door!"

Milkshake flicked her tail. "The laundry room? Do you mean the place with all the humming machines and the scary static shocks? No thanks."

"Come on," Priss said, already moving. "This could be the break we need."

As the animals made their way out of the apartment, Alice cast one last glance at Mrs. Higgins. The woman was now gently rocking, humming a song about casseroles and betrayal.

This mystery was far from over—but now they had a trail to follow.

Shall we head into Chapter 4: Tails and Whispers next?

CHAPTER 4:
TAILS AND WHISKERS

The laundry room at Whisperbrook Apartments was not for the faint of heart. It was full of strange mechanical beasts, growling dryers, spinning washers, and the ever-lurking smell of mystery socks.

"I don't like it here," Milkshake whispered, hopping onto a shelf to avoid touching the cold tile floor. "It smells like burnt lint and human despair."

"Perfect place to hide something," Priss said, nose twitching. "Or someone."

Pretzel was already halfway under a laundry cart, tail wagging at lightning speed. "The trail definitely came this way! I smell tuna, dust bunnies, and—oooh—dryer sheets!"

Alice stayed close to the wall, her sharp eyes scanning every corner. "Let's not forget: this room connects to the ventilation crawlspace. If someone wanted to move around unnoticed, they could."

"You mean... someone used the vents?" Milkshake's ears perked. "Now that's a dramatic getaway. I approve."

Just then, a low growl echoed from behind the dryers.

All four animals froze.

Another growl. A scratch. Then—"Hey! You can't just hog the good napping spots!"

A head popped out from between the machines. It belonged to Trixie, the calico kitten from Unit 2C. Her eyes were wide, and her fur was fluffed out like a fuzzy dandelion.

"Trixie?" Priss asked. "What are you doing back there?"

"Napping!" Trixie huffed. "Until that rude raccoon barged in last night!"

"Raccoon?" Alice said, ears swiveling. "What raccoon?"

"The one that came out of the vent dropped something smelly and vanished again!" Trixie said. "He muttered something about 'getting even' and 'not enough sauce' and then left. I didn't stick around."

Pretzel gasped. "A raccoon! That's a major suspect!"

Milkshake tilted her head. "Revenge. Missing casserole. A vent-hopping raccoon with a grudge. Oh, it's all coming together now."

Alice nodded. "We need more intel. Time to talk to the grapevine."

"The plant?" Pretzel asked, confused.

"No, the network," Priss said. "The animal grapevine. The whispers. The gossip. Time to visit the courtyard."

They left the laundry room behind, following a narrow hallway that led to the building's central courtyard. It was a haven for neighborhood pets, a place where rumors fluttered like bird feathers.

The moment they stepped outside, they were greeted by a chorus of chattering:

"I heard it was the ferret from 1A!"

"No way, it was that sneaky squirrel again!"

"I saw a ghost cat carry something shiny up the fire escape!"

The furry four gathered in the middle of the courtyard.

"Alright," Priss said. "One at a time. We need actual clues, not conspiracy theories."

Just then, a large shadow swooped overhead. It was Professor Featherbottom, the parrot from the penthouse unit. He landed on the wrought iron fence with a dramatic flutter.

"Midnight snack! Sneaky paws! Gone without a trace!" he squawked.

Milkshake arched an eyebrow. "Was that a clue, or just his usual poetry?"

Alice's eyes narrowed. "Let's go ask Ms. Frizzle. She's the only human who understands that birdbrain."

"Do we have time for one more snack break?" Pretzel asked hopefully.

"No," Priss said. "We've got a parrot to interrogate."

And with that, the detectives turned toward the stairs. The mystery deepened with every pawstep, and the whispering grapevine left them with more questions than answers.

One thing was sure: someone had feathers—or fur—in this game, and the furry four were getting closer.

Ready for Chapter 5: Feathered Intel?

CHAPTER 5:
FEATHERED INTEL

The penthouse apartment at Whisperbrook was unlike any other unit in the building. For one, it smelled like sunflower seeds and banana chips. And two, it was home to the eccentric and ever-chipper Ms. Frizzle—the only human who could actually talk to animals.

Well, sort of.

"She listens better than the rest," Alice explained as they padded up the final steps. "Plus, she thinks Featherbottom is a genius. Which… is debatable."

Ms. Frizzle greeted them at the open door in her usual attire: starry-patterned leggings, a feathered headband, and a T-shirt that read "FLUENT IN SQUAWK."

"Oh my stars!" she exclaimed, kneeling to scratch Priss behind the ears. "What a delightful crew. Are we solving another mystery today?"

Milkshake swished her tail. "Technically, yes. Though it might be more accurate to say stumbling through clues while Pretzel knocks over plants."

Pretzel was currently trying to sniff under a decorative throw pillow shaped like a pineapple.

Ms. Frizzle ushered them in. "Featherbottom's been jabbering all morning. I think he saw something."

Professor Featherbottom sat proudly atop his perch by the window. He fluffed his feathers, gave a dramatic cough, and declared:

"Casserole! Midnight! One sneak! One peek!"

Milkshake groaned. "Riddles. Of course."

Ms. Frizzle nodded, eyes wide. "He's been repeating that line over and over since sunrise. I think it's about the missing tuna casserole. Do you think he saw the thief?"

Priss stepped forward. "We think a raccoon might be involved. Maybe one with a grudge."

"Grudge!" Featherbottom squawked. "Sauce scandal! Window sill heist! Gone, gone, GONE!"

Alice's eyes narrowed. "Did you see which window?"

Featherbottom flapped once, then tilted his head toward the courtyard. "Third floor! Clumsy climb! Striped tail! Clack clack claws!"

"A raccoon, alright," Pretzel said, bouncing. "Clack clack claws! That's gotta be him!"

"Anything else?" Priss asked, sitting politely with her ears up.

Featherbottom leaned closer, lowering his voice to a conspiratorial whisper.

"Dropped the dish. Knocked the gnome. Vanished in the vent."

"A vent again!" Milkshake said. "That's twice now."

"And the garden gnome was knocked over?" Priss asked.

"Yep," Ms. Frizzle confirmed. "I found it on its side this morning. Poor Gregory. He's never fallen before."

Alice looked thoughtful. "Then that's our next stop."

"Where?" Pretzel asked.

"The garden," Priss said. "If the raccoon dropped the dish there, we might find paw prints... or better yet, the dish itself."

As the animals turned to leave, Featherbottom gave one last cryptic squawk:

"Fish feast! Sleepy eyes! The truth shall rise!"

They all paused.

Milkshake blinked. "What does that mean?"

Priss was already heading down the stairs. "We'll find out. Come on, team."

Onward to Chapter 6: The Garden Clue?

CHAPTER 6:
THE GARDEN GNOME

Whisperbrook's garden was a well-kept secret—a quiet patch of green tucked behind the apartments, dotted with gnomes, birdbaths, and enough flowers to make any bee faint with joy. It was also the perfect place for a casserole thief to escape.

Priss led the way, her nose twitching like a radar. "Featherbottom said the dish was dropped near the gnome. That would be Gregory, right?"

"I think so," Pretzel said, bounding ahead and skidding to a halt in front of a slightly dirtied gnome with a tilted hat and a disgruntled expression. "Here he is! Poor guy looks traumatized."

"Or just dusty," Milkshake muttered, hopping up onto the garden bench. "Let's find this 'dropped dish' before someone decides it makes a great birdbath."

Alice moved silently along the garden edge. "Over here," she called softly. "Something shiny under the hydrangea bush."

They all rushed over.

There, half-buried in the mulch, was the unmistakable rim of a ceramic casserole dish. It was crusted with a dried bit of golden cheese and smelled faintly of tuna.

"We've got it!" Priss said, tail wagging. "Featherbottom was right!"

Pretzel sniffed it excitedly. "Definitely casserole! And—wait… hold up—raccoon fur!"

Alice examined the dish. "He must've dropped it here when he tried to escape with the whole thing."

"Greedy," Milkshake sniffed. "Didn't even leave leftovers."

Priss tilted her head. "If he came through the vent, crossed the laundry room, and came out here, he must've climbed back up... but where to?"

They all looked up. The garden backed up to the rear of the building, and from here, you could see balconies and fire escapes crisscrossing like a jungle gym.

"That's it," Alice said, nodding toward the old fire escape ladder. "We've got to follow the trail upward."

Pretzel wagged his tail. "Up the fire escape? Adventure!"

"More like potential chaos," Milkshake said, already leaping lightly onto the first rung. "Let's go before it rains or something dramatic happens. Oh wait, that always happens when you say that out loud."

They scaled the fire escape—Priss methodically, Milkshake gracefully, Pretzel chaotically, and Alice with the calm confidence of a cat who'd seen it all before.

From their new perch on the third-floor landing, Alice pointed a paw. "Look. That window's cracked open."

"Mrs. Higgins' bedroom?" Priss asked.

"No," Alice said, eyes narrowing. "That's the spare room. The one she uses for napping."

Milkshake froze. "Wait. Are you saying... she never actually left her apartment?"

Priss blinked. "But we saw her after it went missing!"

"Exactly," Alice said. "But what if she fell asleep before it disappeared?"

Pretzel gasped. "She... she ate it? And then took a nap?!"

"It fits Featherbottom's last clue," Priss murmured. "'Fish feast. Sleepy eyes. The truth shall rise.'"

They all stared at each other.

Then, with the full weight of revelation sinking in, they turned back toward the window.

This case wasn't about a thief.

It was about a nap.

CHAPTER 7:
THE SLEEPY TRUTH

The cracked window let in a soft breeze scented with daisies and forgotten lunch. Priss nosed it open a little wider, and one by one, the furry detectives slipped inside.

The room was cozy and dim, filled with crocheted blankets, teacups stacked on saucers, and a worn armchair nestled beside a sun-drenched window.

And there—snoring lightly beneath a patchwork quilt—was Mrs. Higgins.

"Shhh," Alice whispered. "Let's observe before we accuse anyone of... sleep-eating."

Pretzel crept closer, stepping gently over a knitting project shaped like a confused-looking ferret.

On the floor near the chair was a fork—licked clean—and a crusty corner of what was once unmistakably tuna casserole.

Priss sniffed. "Casserole. Definitely hers."

Milkshake padded closer, flicking her tail in disbelief. "So she made it… took a bite… and never left the room?"

Alice nodded. "The clues all fit. The crumbs in the kitchen? Probably leftovers from her prepping. The dish was moved when she tried to bring it in here; maybe she fumbled it a bit. And the raccoon? He was just scavenging after the fact."

"That's why we hit a dead end!" Priss said. "We were looking for a thief, but there was no crime."

Pretzel's ears drooped. "So… there's no villain?"

"Nope," Alice said with a soft smile. "Just a very satisfied casserole enthusiast who passed out mid-snack."

As if on cue, Mrs. Higgins stirred, blinking sleepily and mumbling, "Mmm… needs more pepper…"

She looked down and saw the four animals sitting in a perfect semi-circle around her chair.

"Oh," she gasped, sitting up with a sleepy chuckle. "Did I… fall asleep again? I made the casserole, had a taste while it cooled… and then I came in here and—oh dear."

She blinked at the fork on the floor. "I suppose I might've eaten the whole thing without realizing it."

Pretzel licked her hand affectionately. "We forgive you."

"Well," Mrs. Higgins said with a warm laugh, "that explains why the dish is empty. I thought someone had taken it!"

Milkshake rolled her eyes. "They did. You."

Mrs. Higgins stood up and shuffled toward the kitchen. "Well, now I feel just terrible. I didn't mean to cause a fuss. I'll make it up to you."

The furry four followed her into the kitchen, where she opened a special drawer and pulled out their favorite treats: salmon bites for the cats, beef jerky cubes for the dogs, and a sprinkle of catnip for good measure.

"You've all been such good little detectives," she said. "Even if the mystery was just me being forgetful and full."

As they munched their rewards, Priss beamed. "We did it, team."

Milkshake licked her paw. "Technically, the only real mystery is how one woman ate an entire casserole alone."

Pretzel burped happily. "This was the best case ever."

Alice curled up in a sunbeam. "Sometimes, the simplest answers are the ones right under our whiskers."

The Whisperbrook mystery had been solved. There were no villains, no grand schemes—just a casserole, a cozy nap, and a team of animal friends closer than ever.

And as the sun set on another quiet evening at the apartment complex, one thing was certain:

The Whisperbrook Detective Agency was always ready... just in case another casserole went missing.

THE WHISPERBROOK DETECTIVE AGENCY SERIES: CASE 2 CURIOUS NEWCOMER

CHAPTER 1:
A STRANGER WITH WHISKERS

Priss was not a fan of surprises. She liked her mornings predictable—wake up, patrol the hallway, sniff the mailroom for clues, and check in on Mrs. Higgins' slippers (just in case they'd wandered off in the night).

But today, something was off.

It started with the scent. Faint but sharp. Like lavender mixed with dust and nervous energy.

Priss wrinkled her nose as she approached Apartment 2C. A crowd of humans had gathered, all talking in high-pitched voices and taking turns crouching to look at a tiny carrier.

Inside was the newcomer.

He was round. Fluffy. And vibrating with anxiety like a fuzzy popcorn kernel on the verge of bursting. He had enormous ears, wide eyes, and a pink nose that twitched every second.

"Ohhh, he's precious!" one of the neighbors gushed.

"He's exotic," said another. "What did they say his name was?"

"Churro," murmured someone. "He's a chinchilla."

Priss's ears perked. She turned to find Pretzel halfway wedged behind a potted plant, watching intently.

"Do chinchillas usually twitch that much?" Pretzel whispered.

"No," Priss said. "But I've got a twitchy feeling myself."

Milkshake arrived next, hopping lightly up onto the railing and peering down. "He smells like pine shavings and secrets."

Alice, as usual, arrived last and calmest. "New pets always bring a little chaos," she said. "We'll give him a day to settle. If he's harmless, we'll know. If he's hiding something... we'll know that, too."

Inside the apartment, the humans placed Churro gently into a spacious enclosure filled with ramps, hay, and a tiny wooden log shaped like a castle. The little chinchilla peeked out, blinking nervously at the world.

Then, quick as a flash, he vanished.

"Did he just teleport?" Pretzel yelped.

"No," Alice said slowly, "he found a tunnel."

"A tunnel?" Priss echoed. "In Whisperbrook?"

Milkshake narrowed her eyes. "Either he's really clever... or he's been here before."

The four detectives shared a glance.

Something wasn't right about the new pet next door.

And they intended to find out exactly what it was.

CHAPTER 2:
VANISHING ACTS

By the next morning, Whisperbrook was buzzing.

Not because of the usual garden gossip or Mrs. Poole's morning kazoo warm-up—no, this time, it was because things were going missing.

Little things, at first.

Milkshake noticed her favorite sunning spot on the windowsill had been mysteriously covered with wood shavings.

Priss found that the tennis ball she kept hidden under the sofa in the common room had vanished without a trace.

And Pretzel? He was still whining about the missing half of his peanut butter biscuit, which he definitely didn't eat himself. Probably.

"I had it under my pillow," he insisted, pacing. "It was my emergency snack!"

Alice simply sipped from the water bowl near the courtyard and said, "Three disappearances in less than a day. Coincidence? I think not."

Milkshake narrowed her eyes toward the second floor. "You think it's the new guy?"

Priss nodded slowly. "New pet arrives, stuff starts disappearing, and he's already found access to tunnels inside the building? Suspicious."

"And quiet," Pretzel added. "Too quiet. He doesn't bark, squeak, or even sneeze. I sneezed six times just this morning!"

Milkshake rolled her eyes. "That's because you rolled in the daffodils."

Still, Priss couldn't shake the feeling something was off. She decided to patrol Churro's hallway. Just observe. Sniff. Listen.

That's when she heard it.

Scraaaaape. Shuffle. Thump.

A soft sound behind the wall between Apartments 2C and 2B.

Priss pressed her nose to the baseboard. "There's a tunnel. I knew it."

She barked once—soft and short—and within minutes, the others had joined her.

Milkshake flicked her tail. "Are we saying Churro has secret tunnels and is using them to hoard our stuff?"

"Possibly," Alice murmured. "Or he's running from something."

Pretzel's ears perked up. "You mean he's not just a thief—he's a fugitive?!"

"Let's not jump to conclusions," Priss said. "We need proof."

Just then, a small puff of dust floated up from the baseboard. A tiny, furry face appeared from the shadows, Churro.

He froze when he saw them, blinked twice…

…and bolted back into the wall.

"Oh, he's hiding something," Milkshake hissed.

Priss growled softly. "Let's follow him."

The Whisperbrook Detective Agency had a new mission: find out what Churro was hiding.

And whether he was just scared…

…or something else…

CHAPTER 3:
TUNNELS

"I don't like small spaces," Pretzel muttered as he stared at the hole Churro disappeared into. "What if I get stuck? What if there are spiders? What if—"

"Pretzel," Milkshake cut in, "you once tried to dig your way into the freezer for ice cream. You'll be fine."

Alice calmly stepped forward and nudged the baseboard panel with her paw. It wobbled, then gave way with a click.

A small tunnel revealed itself—lined with dust, a few suspicious peanut shells, and tufts of fur that didn't belong to anyone currently living at Whisperbrook.

"Let's go," Priss said, crouching low and squeezing inside. The tunnel was narrow but not too tight for a determined corgi.

Milkshake followed with elegant ease. Alice slinked behind like she'd lived in the walls for years.

Pretzel whimpered once, then shoved his way in with a grunt.

The air was cool and smelled of old wallpaper and secrets. The tunnel branched left and right, zigzagging between apartments like a forgotten maze.

"This explains how Churro's been getting around unnoticed," Milkshake whispered.

Alice nodded. "These tunnels were probably part of the building's old heating system. Long sealed off… but not for a chinchilla clever enough to find them."

They followed the trail—marked by wood shavings, the occasional dropped raisin, and… what was that?

Priss paused and sniffed a pile of debris. "My tennis ball!" she gasped, tugging it free from under a discarded sock.

"And that's my biscuit!" Pretzel yelped, pouncing on it. "Only slightly dusty!"

Milkshake narrowed her eyes. "He's building a stash. But why? Just for snacks?"

Alice stopped suddenly. "No," she said, her voice low. "Look ahead."

They all peered through a small wooden slat and saw it—a hidden nook tucked between the walls. Churro was there, sitting on a small pile of stolen trinkets: shiny buttons, shredded paper, food wrappers, and a squeaky toy missing its squeak.

But he wasn't lounging. He was... shivering.

Next to him, wrapped in a scarf like a blanket, was a second chinchilla. Smaller. Even twitchier. Eyes closed.

"A baby?" Pretzel whispered.

"No," Alice said gently. "A sibling."

Priss's heart sank.

Churro wasn't a thief.

He was protecting someone.

CHAPTER 4: SECRETS IN THE SHADOWS

For a moment, no one spoke.

Even Pretzel was completely still—his usual bouncy energy replaced by wide eyes and a tilted head.

Inside the nook, Churro gently placed a dried blueberry next to the smaller chinchilla, then curled around them protectively. His tiny ears twitched as he stared back through the slats, eyes wide with fear.

"He's not stealing for himself," Alice said softly. "He's scavenging for his sibling."

Milkshake narrowed her eyes. "Then why not tell someone? Why sneak around?"

"Because he's scared," Priss whispered. "He probably doesn't trust anyone yet. Especially not in a brand-new place."

Pretzel sniffled. "They're... really small."

"And Whisperbrook can feel really big when you're alone," Alice added.

Just then, a soft creak came from the hallway above. The humans. They were moving around—calling for Churro, knocking on walls, probably realizing something wasn't quite right.

"We need to do something," Priss said. "We can't just watch."

Alice nodded. "We introduce ourselves. The right way."

Milkshake gave her paw a quick lick. "With diplomacy."

"And snacks," Pretzel added quickly. "Snacks are always good."

Priss gently pushed open a slat at the base of the nook, making just enough space for her nose. She stepped inside slowly, tail wagging low and calm.

"Hey there," she said softly. "We're not here to take anything back. We just want to help."

Churro tensed, placing himself in front of his sibling.

"We're part of the neighborhood watch," Milkshake said smoothly as she slipped in behind Priss. "The unofficial, highly qualified, four-pawed kind."

Alice padded in next, her tone gentle and wise. "You're safe now, little ones. Whisperbrook isn't perfect… but it is home. And we take care of our own."

Churro hesitated.

Then, slowly—so slowly—he stepped back, just a little. Enough to show trust. Enough to allow them closer.

Pretzel squeezed in last, dragging a half-melted cheese cube with him. "Snack?"

The tiniest whiskers twitched from under the scarf. A soft squeak came in reply.

Churro's sibling was awake.

They were safe. Still scared—but not alone.

Not anymore.

CHAPTER 5:
NEIGHBORS FOR REAL

Later that afternoon, the sun spilt through the windows of Whisperbrook Apartments, warming the floorboards and filling the halls with a golden glow.

The kind of glow that made you feel like things might just be okay.

The Whisperbrook Detective Agency—now temporarily acting as the Welcome Committee—led Churro and his little sibling (whose name, it turned out, was Nilla) out of the tunnels and into the world above.

Churro trembled with every step.

Nilla peeked out from a pouch made from Pretzel's old sock, clinging to her brother's fur.

But the others walked with them, slow and proud.

As they reached Apartment 2C, Ms. Frizzle stood at the door, eyes wide and teary.

"Oh my stars!" she gasped. "There you are! I was so worried!"

She crouched down as Churro stopped at her feet. He looked up nervously.

But Ms. Frizzle didn't scold. She didn't shout. She simply opened her arms.

Churro hesitated.

Then, with a tiny squeak, he nuzzled into her hand.

"Welcome home, sweet boy," she whispered. "And you, little one."

Nilla peeked up from her sock-pouch and gave a tiny sneeze.

The humans never did find out where the missing biscuit, the tennis ball, or the squeaky toy went.

But no one minded.

Later that evening, Mrs. Higgins threw a "Welcome to Whisperbrook" party in the courtyard. There were crunchy treats for the dogs, tuna bits for the cats, and a special tray of dried fruit and hay for the chinchillas.

Churro and Nilla sat close together under a flower pot, watching quietly.

Eventually, Churro crept forward and placed a shiny button on Priss's paw.

"A gift," Alice whispered. "A thank-you."

Priss wagged her tail gently. "We're glad you're here."

Pretzel bounded over, dropping a peanut near Nilla. "Official Whisperbrook snack protocol!"

Milkshake gave Churro a single nod of approval. "You've got guts, whiskers."

The stars came out one by one above the courtyard.

And for the first time, Churro didn't feel like a stranger.

He felt like a neighbor.

EPILOGUE:
THE WHISPER BROOK WAY

Life at Whisperbrook settled into its usual rhythm, mostly peaceful, occasionally peculiar, and always full of stories.

Churro and Nilla quickly became part of the fabric of the building. The humans adored them, often pausing in the hallway to coo and offer snacks. The animals… well, they watched out for them in their own ways.

Priss added an "Emergency Chinchilla Protocol" to her patrol schedule.

Milkshake offered fashion advice—though she swore she was not emotionally invested.

Pretzel appointed himself their "Big Bark Brother," promising to chase away any ghost, shadow, or suspicious houseplant.

Alice—wise as ever—taught them the secret napping spots only the oldest residents knew.

As for the tunnels? Sealed by the humans… mostly. But one panel near the laundry room stayed just loose enough, just in case.

Because Whisperbrook wasn't just a place; it was a home.

A home where mysteries were solved not with force but with kindness.

Where strangers became friends.

And where every creaky hallway, every flickering light, and every whisper of wind carried the promise that no matter what the mystery…the Whisperbrook Detective Agency was on the case.

THE WHISPERBROOK DETECTIVE AGENCY SERIES: CASE 3 VANISHING ACT

CHAPTER 1:
NO SIGN OF ALICE

The day started like any other.

Milkshake was sunning herself in the window of Apartment 3A, ears twitching lazily as birds chirped outside. Priss was on her usual hallway patrol, sniffing every doormat for signs of trouble (or dropped crumbs). Pretzel was trying—again—to balance three squeaky toys on his nose.

But something was off.

No one had seen Alice that morning.

Not by the garden window where she usually sipped water. Not curled up on her pillow in Apartment 1B. Not even by the radiator in the lobby—her favorite winter nap spot.

"She's probably napping somewhere new," Pretzel offered half-heartedly. "Cats do that. Right?"

"Not Alice," Priss said firmly. "She sticks to routines like glue. If she changed it, there's a reason."

Milkshake flicked her tail. "And she never misses breakfast with Mrs. Higgins."

"Never," Priss echoed.

That's when the door to Apartment 1B creaked open. Mrs. Higgins leaned out, worry etched across her face.

"Have any of you seen Alice?" she called to the hallway. "She didn't come home last night."

A chill settled over the Whisperbrook pets.

Alice, the wisest and oldest among them, was missing.

And if Alice was in trouble... something serious was going on.

Milkshake narrowed her eyes. "Get the team."

Priss's tail stiffened. "We're on the case."

Pretzel dropped his toys and gave a determined bark. "Detectives, assemble!"

Because when a Whisperbrook resident goes missing, the Whisperbrook Detective Agency is on the case.

CHAPTER 2:
THE CLUE IN THE COURTYARD

The Whisperbrook courtyard was quiet that morning—too quiet.

Usually, you could hear the hum of Mrs. Poole watering her ferns or Mr. Jenkins arguing with his radio. Today, just the rustle of leaves and the faint rattle of the wind chimes near Apartment 1B.

Priss led the way, nose low to the ground. "We'll start where she was last seen. Mrs. Higgins said Alice went for her usual moonlight stroll around the courtyard last night. Never came back."

"Maybe she got stuck in a hedge," Pretzel suggested hopefully, bounding ahead and sniffing a row of rosebushes. "Or maybe she found a squirrel tunnel and decided to become queen of the squirrels!"

Milkshake rolled her eyes. "If Alice joined a squirrel kingdom, we'd all be hearing about it by now."

They reached the center of the courtyard, where a cracked stone birdbath stood surrounded by ivy.

Priss paused, sniffing hard.

"Something… fishy," she muttered.

Milkshake perked up. "Fishy as in tuna? Or suspicious?"

"Both," Priss replied. She nudged a loose brick at the base of the birdbath—and a glint of something shiny caught the light.

Milkshake padded closer. "That's Alice's collar bell."

Priss gently pawed it free. "Still warm. It wasn't here long."

Pretzel's ears drooped. "So... she didn't wander off. She left something behind."

Alice would never lose her bell on purpose. She was precise. Careful. Always aware.

"She left it as a signal," Milkshake said. "A clue."

Priss's eyes narrowed. "But a signal for what?"

Just then, a soft flutter echoed above. A sharp squawk followed.

"Shadows in the ivy! Secrets in stone!"

They all looked up to see Professor Featherbottom—Ms. Frizzle's parrot—perched on the balcony railing, bobbing his head.

"Was that...?" Pretzel began.

"Clue number two," Milkshake said, tail swishing. "Let's pay a visit to the professor."

Because Alice's disappearance wasn't an accident.

She left a trail.

And the Whisperbrook Detective Agency was going to follow it.

CHAPTER 3:
SECRETS FROM THE SKY

The door to Apartment 4C creaked open just enough to let the team slip inside—well, everyone except Pretzel, who had to wiggle through sideways after knocking over an umbrella stand.

Professor Featherbottom was already waiting, perched dramatically on the back of Ms. Frizzle's favorite armchair, one clawed foot gripping a cracker, the other tapping a rhythm only he understood.

"State your business," he croaked. "No nonsense. No muffins."

Priss stepped forward. "We think Alice left us a clue before she disappeared. You mentioned 'shadows in the ivy' and 'secrets in stone.' What does that mean?"

Featherbottom puffed up his feathers, blinked once, then turned in a slow circle. "She whispered a rhyme," he said gravely. "Just after sunset."

"Alice talked to you?" Milkshake asked, surprised.

Featherbottom nodded. "Not talk. Poem."

Pretzel's tail wagged, hopefully. "I love poems!"

"She said," Featherbottom began, his voice soft now, "'Where ivy creeps, and secrets sleep, the wall shall show the path that's deep.'"

The room went quiet.

Milkshake broke the silence first. "That's definitely Alice. Mysterious and annoyingly poetic."

Priss was already pacing. "So she meant the ivy in the courtyard. Maybe there's a hidden path—or something behind the wall."

Featherbottom added, "She carried a small pouch. Hidden. Heavy."

"A pouch?" Pretzel echoed. "Like... a treasure pouch?!"

"She tucked it in the stone wall," the parrot confirmed. "Then vanished into the ivy."

Milkshake's tail twitched. "Then that's where we go next. We search that wall from moss to mortar."

Priss nodded. "If Alice left something behind, she wanted us to find it."

"And if there's a hidden path..." Pretzel grinned. "I definitely want to fall into it!"

Professor Featherbottom bobbed his head. "Hurry. The ivy whispers. The shadows are moving."

Priss turned to the team. "We've got a poem, a pouch, and a parrot's warning."

Milkshake flicked her whiskers. "Let's get back to the courtyard. Alice's trail isn't cold yet."

And with that, the Whisperbrook Detective Agency raced downstairs—toward ivy, stone, and the mystery waiting in the walls.

CHAPTER 4:
THE HIDDEN HOLLOW

The ivy wall behind the birdbath looked ordinary enough unless you were a seasoned detective with a sharp nose and an even sharper mind.

Luckily, Whisperbrook had both.

Priss sniffed along the stones, tail stiff with focus. "There's something behind this patch," she murmured, brushing aside a thick strand of ivy with her paw.

Milkshake narrowed her eyes. "That stone's different. Slightly loose. Alice must've pulled it out."

Pretzel bounded forward, already wedging his nose into the gap. "Allow me!" he barked and, with an enthusiastic wiggle—knocked the stone clean out of the wall.

Inside, nestled in a dark nook, was a tiny cloth pouch tied with a red ribbon.

Priss gently pulled it out and opened it with a nudge of her snout.

Milkshake peered in. "That's… catnip?"

"And string. And—wait—is that a folded piece of paper?" Priss tugged it free and spread it on the ground.

The note was written in elegant ink, clearly Alice's pawwork. It read:

"If I'm not home by moonrise, follow the old scent beneath the stone steps. The truth lies where the earth hums."

Pretzel tilted his head. "Okay… that sounds spooky."

Milkshake's voice was quiet. "It sounds like she knew something. Something big."

"Something dangerous," Priss added.

They all looked toward the far end of the courtyard—where a crumbling stone staircase led down to the old, unused laundry cellar. It had been boarded up for years.

Or so everyone thought.

A breeze rustled the ivy.

Milkshake stood. "Moonrise isn't far off."

"We follow the scent," Priss said, already trotting toward the steps.

Pretzel bounced after them, the pouch swinging from his mouth. "Wait for me! I've got snacks!"

As they reached the stone stairs, the ground felt cooler—older somehow. The scent in the air changed, and the hum of something beneath whispered through their paws.

Alice had been here.

And if she'd gone underground, she'd had a reason.

The Whisperbrook Detective Agency descended the steps, one by one, into the shadows.

Whatever was hidden down there—it was time to find out.

CHAPTER 5:
BENEATH WHISPERBROOK

The stone steps creaked beneath their paws as the team crept into the dark.

Pretzel sneezed. "It smells like socks. And… secrets."

The cellar was bigger than they'd imagined—long and low, with ancient pipes curling like vines along the ceiling. Dust danced in the thin beams of light that poked through cracks above. At the far end, part of the brick wall had crumbled away, leaving a small opening barely big enough for a cat—or a corgi—to squeeze through.

"That must be where she went," Milkshake whispered.

Priss crouched and sniffed the ground. "Fresh pawprints. One set. Definitely Alice."

They followed the tracks through the narrow opening and into a hidden chamber beyond.

And there—curled up beneath an old storage shelf, eyes blinking against the light—was Alice.

"Alice!" Pretzel yipped, rushing forward.

She lifted her head slowly, and a small, tired smile crept across her face. "You found me."

Milkshake was already checking her over. "Are you okay? What happened?"

Alice stretched carefully, a bit stiff. "I came down here to follow a scent I hadn't smelled in years. Something… familiar. From before Whisperbrook. I didn't want to worry anyone unless it was something real."

"And was it?" Priss asked.

Alice nodded slowly. "Someone—or something—has been in the tunnels. Watching. Listening. I found signs. Scratches. Nesting fur. Too big for a mouse. Too clever to be alone."

The team went still.

"A stowaway?" Milkshake asked.

"Or a spy," Alice said, her eyes narrowing.

Pretzel gulped. "A spy squirrel?!"

Alice didn't laugh.

"There's something strange going on beneath this building," she said softly. "Something that didn't come from Whisperbrook. And now that we've found each other, we need to find it."

Priss helped her to her feet. "You could've told us."

"I knew you'd follow the clues," Alice said, brushing a bit of dust off her fur. "You're detectives, after all."

Milkshake smirked. "Well, don't get used to the dramatic exits."

Pretzel wagged his tail. "Let's get out of here. You're coming home."

Together, the Whisperbrook Detective Agency turned back toward the tunnel entrance, the mystery deepening around them like the shadows on the walls.

Alice was safe—but this case was far from over.

Here's Chapter 6: Back Upstairs, the final chapter of The Case of the Vanishing Veteran:

CHAPTER 6:
BACK UPSTAIRS

The sun was just beginning to set when the Whisperbrook Detective Agency emerged from the cellar. The air was warmer up here, filled with the scent of blooming jasmine and the soft rustle of curtains in the open windows.

Alice blinked against the light, stretching as she stepped into the courtyard.

"Home," she murmured. "Never looked so good."

Mrs. Higgins was already waiting near the birdbath, her face brightening when she saw her oldest companion. "Alice! Oh, thank goodness!"

Alice padded forward with dignity, accepting a scoop-up into Mrs. Higgins' arms with quiet grace. "I didn't mean to scare you," she said softly.

Mrs. Higgins pressed her cheek to Alice's fur. "You gave me quite the fright, old girl."

Priss sat tall and proud beside the ivy wall. "Case closed," she said.

"Not quite," Alice corrected, looking at her fellow detectives. "There's more happening below Whisperbrook than any of us thought. But we'll take it one case at a time."

Milkshake yawned, flicking her tail. "After a nap, maybe."

Pretzel flopped on the grass. "And snacks. Lots of snacks."

Professor Featherbottom squawked from above. "No muffins! No muffins!"

Alice smiled. "Thank you, team. You didn't just find me—you followed every clue, trusted each other, and showed true courage."

Priss tilted her head. "So what was really down there?"

"I'm not sure yet," Alice admitted. "But I think we've got a new neighbor. A quiet one. A sneaky one."

Milkshake purred. "Sounds like our kind of mystery."

As the stars twinkled overhead and the apartment lights glowed golden against the night, the Whisperbrook Detective Agency curled up in their usual spots—watchful, curious, and ready.

Because even in the quietest corners of Whisperbrook Apartments, the adventure never sleeps for long.

THE END or is it?

THE WHISPERBROOK DETECTIVE AGENCY SERIES: CASE 4 MIDNIGHT HOWL

CHAPTER 1:
MIDNIGHT MOON

It started with a sound.

Low. Long. Sad.

"Arooooooooo..."

The howl floated through the vents and stairwells of Whisperbrook Apartments like a ghost with nowhere to go. It was exactly midnight. Every night. For the past three nights.

The humans barely noticed. They'd chalked it up to creaky pipes or a lonely dog two blocks away.

But the animals knew better.

"I heard it again last night," Priss said, pacing the hallway outside Apartment 4C. "Third time. Right at midnight."

"It echoed through the radiator," Milkshake added, perching on a windowsill. "It gave Mr. Pickles the chinchilla a full-body shiver."

Pretzel rolled onto his back, all four paws in the air. "What if it's a ghost dog?" he asked, not sounding nearly as scared as he should've.

Alice's voice came from her usual spot on the stairwell landing. "No dog I've known ever howled like that. Too long. Too lonely."

They all went quiet.

Whisperbrook had seen its share of strange happenings—missing casseroles, secret tunnels, cats who left cryptic poems—but this was something different. Something... eerie.

"We need to find the source," Priss said, determined. "If it's a lost pet, they need help. If it's a ghost... well, we'll deal with that too."

Milkshake flicked her tail. "I'll check the fire escape. The sound echoed off the metal."

"Pretzel and I will sniff the main hallway," Priss added. "Alice?"

"I'll talk to the mice," Alice said calmly. "They hear everything."

They nodded in agreement. The Whisperbrook Detective Agency was officially on the case.

And as the moon crept across the sky, the four detectives split up—each chasing the same question:

Who was howling at midnight—and why?

CHAPTER 2:
TRACKS IN THE DUST

The basement hallway was still, too, still.

Priss's nails clicked softly against the tile floor as she sniffed along the wall, her corgi nose low and alert. Pretzel trotted behind her, tail swishing excitedly.

"Do ghosts leave pawprints?" he whispered.

"No," Priss answered, "but lost dogs do."

They turned the corner near the boiler room and stopped in their tracks.

There—etched faintly into a patch of dusty floor—were pawprints. Not cat-sized. Bigger. Clawed. Uneven.

Priss lowered her head to sniff. "Fresh. Maybe just a few hours old."

Pretzel squinted. "That one has a smudge in it. Like they limped a little?"

Priss nodded. "Whoever it is, they're not just wandering. They're trying to stay hidden."

Suddenly, a pipe above them let out a soft clang, and the lights flickered. Both dogs jumped.

"I wasn't scared," Pretzel said quickly. "Just, um, stretching."

Priss didn't reply. She was staring at the wall.

One of the basement vents was open—just slightly. And next to it, something shiny caught her eye.

She padded over and nudged it gently. A small, rusted dog tag lay half-buried in the dust. The name was scratched up, but a few letters remained:

"…O…E…"

"Is that a clue?" Pretzel asked.

Priss tucked it carefully under her collar. "It's more than that. It's a name."

Footsteps echoed above them—human ones this time. A door creaked open. The detectives froze.

"Come on," Priss whispered. "We've got prints, a tag, and a trail to follow."

Pretzel bounced after her. "Do you think the others found something, too?"

Priss looked back at the open vent. "I hope so. Because we're not just chasing a sound anymore."

CHAPTER 3:
RECON

The moon was high and full, casting silver light across the rooftop of Whisperbrook Apartments.

Milkshake leapt silently from one ledge to another, tail flicking like a metronome. Her fur shimmered in the moonlight as she crept toward the corner where the howling always seemed to echo loudest.

She paused beside the old chimney vent, sniffing the air.

"Smoke. Rust. And…"

She froze.

"Wet fur."

The scent wasn't old. It was fresh—still warm in the air like someone had passed through minutes ago.

From her perch, she scanned the surrounding rooftops. Across the alley, an old garage sat with a flat, mossy roof. And on that roof, half-hidden in shadow, something moved.

Milkshake's eyes narrowed.

A shape—medium-sized. Low to the ground. Pacing in circles. Then pausing.

It raised its head and—

"Aroooooooo…"

The same howl. Right on time.

Milkshake's fur bristled. She crouched lower and watched. The creature didn't look dangerous… just lost. Its howl was full of longing.

Then, as suddenly as it appeared, the shadowy figure darted out of view—leaping from the garage roof and disappearing into the alley below.

Milkshake let out a sharp meow—the signal. Seconds later, a small voice crackled from a nearby vent. It was Professor Featherbottom, squawking into Ms. Frizzle's walkie-talkie perch inside.

"Midnight activity confirmed! The subject is mobile. I repeat—mobile!"

Milkshake turned back toward the fire escape. "Time to report in," she muttered. "And time to find out who—or what—is keeping our nights from sleeping."

CHAPTER 4:
THE WHISPER IN THE VENT

The air in the hallway was thick with mystery as Priss and Pretzel made their way back to the apartments. The basement seemed further behind them now, but the trail wasn't just in the dust—it was in the air. The lingering scent of that lost dog, the rusted dog tag, and the strange pawprints—it all led them back up to the apartments themselves.

"Think we missed anything?" Pretzel asked, hopping over a small pile of laundry.

"I don't think so," Priss replied, scanning every corner. "But the howling is only half of it. It's like something—or someone—is trying to communicate with us."

She stopped in front of the vent in the hallway. A faint breeze whistled from the ducts.

"That's what's bothering me," she said softly, sniffing at the metal grate. "The sound seems to come from here."

Pretzel sniffed the floor. "It smells like… metal? And, uh, something else."

Priss leaned closer. "It's like there's a message hiding in the noise."

Just then, a soft voice came from above them—a faint whisper that could barely be heard.

"Help me…"

Priss stood up straight, ears pricked. "Did you hear that?"

Pretzel blinked. "Did… did it come from the vent?"

Before Priss could answer, the floor beneath them trembled lightly. It wasn't much—just a slight vibration—but enough to make them both freeze.

"Something's moving in the walls," Priss said, her voice low.

"We need to get to the source," Pretzel replied, his tail wagging with excitement. "I've always wanted to chase something inside a wall!"

Priss rolled her eyes. "I hope it's not a squirrel. Or worse, a rat."

The whisper came again, clearer this time, like a voice from far away.

"Help me..."

The two detectives exchanged a glance. There was no doubt now—the sound wasn't a coincidence. Someone—or something—was trying to reach them from within the walls of Whisperbrook Apartments.

"Let's go," Priss said, determination in her eyes. "We're going to follow that whisper and find out what's hiding inside this building."

Pretzel grinned. "And maybe finally get to the bottom of the howl!"

CHAPTER 5:
THE ALLEY

The moon hung low, casting long shadows over the narrow alley beside Whisperbrook Apartments. The wind rustled the leaves of the overgrown ivy that clung to the brick walls, making everything seem a little more mysterious—more alive.

Priss and Pretzel padded silently down the alley, the night air cool against their fur. They had followed the trail up to the rooftops, but now they were back on the ground, sniffing for any other signs that could help them unravel the mystery.

"I don't like it," Priss muttered. "Too quiet."

Pretzel's tail was low, almost dragging along the ground. "I've got a bad feeling. Do you think it could be something... dangerous?"

Priss stopped and sniffed the air, her nose twitching. "I don't know yet. But it feels like someone—or something—has been down here recently."

They paused beneath a streetlight, its flickering glow casting eerie shadows around them.

That's when Pretzel's ears perked up.

"Wait—do you hear that?"

The faintest scratching sound reached their ears. It came from further down the alley, near a large pile of old crates and discarded furniture. Something was moving. Something small. Something that didn't want to be seen.

"Let's check it out," Priss said, her voice a whisper.

Pretzel didn't need any more encouragement. He darted forward, nose to the ground. As they got closer, they saw a flash of movement in the shadows.

Then, a loud thunk echoed as something jumped off a pile of crates and landed softly on the ground. Priss's eyes narrowed.

"Gotcha," she murmured.

From the darkness, a small creature emerged—its coat gray and dusty, with wide, suspicious eyes. It was a raccoon.

"Whoa there!"

CHAPTER 6:
UNDER THE MOON

The drainpipes of Whisperbrook Apartments loomed before them, twisted and dark, like veins leading deep into the heart of the building. The small grate near the edge of the alley had been pried open, revealing a small, dark opening.

Priss stood tall, staring down into the inky darkness. "This is it. The howling's coming from down there. But why?" she murmured, looking at Pretzel.

Pretzel wagged his tail, practically bouncing with excitement. "It's like a secret underground lair! Maybe we'll find treasure!"

Priss gave him a quick, thoughtful look. "Or we'll find exactly what's causing the noise. Either way, we need to be careful."

Milkshake, who had joined them after her rooftop reconnaissance, hopped up beside them, her eyes narrowed with concentration. "I think we're all missing the point here. Something or someone is trying to get to us through the walls. That howl isn't just a cry for help. It's a message."

Alice appeared from the shadows, her eyes glowing in the dark. "And if anyone can solve this, it's all of us together," she said with quiet wisdom. "Let's go."

Together, they descended into the drainpipe, carefully navigating the steep, slippery slope. The air grew cooler and thicker as they moved deeper, and the faint sound of dripping water echoed in the tight space. The walls felt close, and each step seemed to lead them further into the unknown.

Finally, after what felt like hours, the passage opened up into a cavernous, abandoned space beneath the apartments. The walls were lined with old pipes, and the smell of mildew was heavy in the air.

Priss's eyes scanned the room. There was a strange, unsettling feeling that swept over her. "We're close," she whispered, her ears perked up. "This place feels... wrong."

Pretzel sniffed the air. "I smell something familiar," he said, wrinkling his nose. "But I can't place it."

"Shh," Milkshake hissed, her fur standing on end. "There's something moving."

The shadows seemed to shift, and then, from behind a large stack of old crates, a pair of glowing eyes appeared. The figure stepped forward, revealing itself in the dim light.

It was a large, shaggy dog—bigger than any of them had seen. Its fur was matted, and its eyes were full of sadness. The howling had stopped.

"Are you... the one who's been howling?" Priss asked, stepping forward cautiously.

The dog tilted its head, its eyes filled with a mix of fear and confusion. It let out a low whine. "I didn't mean to scare anyone. I just... I just wanted to go home," the dog said, its voice quiet and shaky.

Milkshake's tail flicked with sympathy. "Home? What happened?"

The dog lowered its head, avoiding their gazes. "I used to live here, in Whisperbrook. I was part of a family, once. But... they moved away, and I was left behind. I couldn't leave. I couldn't find my way out."

Priss's heart softened. "You were the one howling."

The dog nodded. "I wanted to be heard. I wanted someone to find me. But I didn't know how to ask for help."

Alice stepped forward, her voice gentle. "You've been hiding down here, in the shadows. You've been lost and afraid. But you don't have to be anymore. We'll help you."

The large dog's eyes brightened, and for the first time, a faint wag of its tail appeared. "You would... help me?"

"Of course we will," Pretzel said, bounding over excitedly. "Everyone deserves a home."

Milkshake gave the dog a soft, knowing smile. "And maybe you'll find a new family here at Whisperbrook."

Priss took a deep breath, her eyes scanning the room. "But we can't let you stay here. It's too dangerous. We'll get you back to the surface. You don't belong in these dark corners."

With the dog nodding in agreement, they led him back toward the drainpipe and back to the surface. The full moon greeted them once more as they emerged from the shadows.

As they stepped back into the fresh air, the dog looked at the group with a renewed sense of hope. "I can't thank you enough," it said softly. "I was so afraid no one would ever find me."

Priss smiled. "You're part of Whisperbrook now. No one gets left behind."

The night seemed quieter now as if the building itself had released the weight of the long, haunting howl. And in the distance, a soft, distant bark echoed—a happy, content sound, just like the start of a new chapter for both the dog and the Whisperbrook Detective Agency.

CHAPTER 7:
RETURN

The first rays of dawn began to peek over the horizon as the team of detectives walked back toward Whisperbrook Apartments. The large dog, now identified as Samson, trotted beside them with a newfound bounce in his step. He was no longer the quiet, fearful figure they'd first encountered. He was full of hope and gratitude.

As they reached the front doors of Whisperbrook, Samson stopped. His tail wagged uncertainly. "This is it, isn't it?" he asked. "I really get to stay here?"

Priss gave him a reassuring nod. "You're not alone anymore, Samson. We'll make sure you're safe and comfortable."

Milkshake padded up beside him, her eyes soft. "Whisperbrook might not have been kind to you before, but we'll change that. It's a place for all kinds of families—human or animal."

Samson looked around, his eyes scanning the building with a mix of uncertainty and excitement. "I don't want to be a bother."

Pretzel bounced around in circles, tail wagging furiously. "No way! You're a part of our crew now. No one gets left behind here."

Alice, who had been walking in quiet contemplation, stopped beside the group. Her wise, amber eyes focused on Samson. "Home isn't just about where you sleep. It's about where you belong. And you, Samson, belong here."

The air seemed lighter as if the building itself had sighed with relief.

Just then, the door to Mrs. Higgins' apartment creaked open, and the elderly woman stepped out, her large glasses perched on her nose. Her ever-present cat, Mrs. Whiskers, was on her shoulder, eyes narrowing as she took in the scene.

"Well, what do we have here?" Mrs. Higgins asked, eyeing Samson with curiosity. "A new resident?"

Before anyone could answer, Mrs. Whiskers gave a haughty meow and stretched on Mrs. Higgins' shoulder. "About time you showed up. I was starting to get bored with my nightly surveillance," she remarked, giving Samson a dismissive glance.

Samson lowered his head a little, unsure how to respond.

Mrs. Higgins, however, stepped forward with a kind smile. "If you're staying here, you're more than welcome, dear. We could use some extra paws around here." She turned to the detectives with a twinkle in her eye. "Looks like you've solved yet another mystery. You're quite the team."

Milkshake padded over to Mrs. Higgins, flicking her tail with a soft purr. "We couldn't have done it without you."

The elderly woman chuckled softly, reaching down to give Milkshake a light scratch behind the ears. "I suspect that, yes."

With the mystery of the howling resolved and Samson now a part of Whisperbrook's unique community, the detectives took a moment to reflect on what they had uncovered.

The howls, once a source of fear and confusion, were now a thing of the past. Whisperbrook Apartments was a little less haunted and a lot more whole.

"Another case closed," Priss said, her chest puffing up with pride.

Pretzel barked in agreement, spinning in a circle. "And a new friend gained!"

Milkshake, always cool and collected, gave a soft nod. "Let's just hope the next mystery isn't so loud."

Alice smiled to herself as she watched the new team of friends settling into their roles. "Every mystery is important. But the real challenge is making sure no one ever feels alone."

Samson sat down with a contented sigh. "I think I've found my home."

And as the first full light of the day filled the hallway, the detectives—new and old—knew that whatever mystery came next, they would solve it together.

CHAPTER 8:
THE QUIET NIGHT

The sun had fully risen now, casting a golden hue over Whisperbrook Apartments. The once tense and eerie atmosphere of the past few nights had lifted. The hallway, once filled with mysterious sounds, now hummed with the normal, peaceful rhythm of apartment life.

Inside Mrs. Higgins' apartment, the new family had gathered for a quiet celebration. A batch of Mrs. Higgins' famous tuna casserole sat on the table, steam rising gently from the dish.

"This is for all of you," Mrs. Higgins said, smiling warmly at the group of detectives gathered around her. "I'm so grateful for your help. You brought this old dog back to his home."

Samson sat at the foot of the table, his tail wagging lazily as he looked around at his new family. His eyes sparkled with joy, and he had never looked more content. The detectives, all seated at the table, shared a moment of peace, knowing the case was finally solved.

"Seems like we're all a bit of a family now," Pretzel said with a wag of his tail. "And who knows? Maybe this is just the start of more mysteries."

Priss gave him a playful nudge. "Let's hope not too many mysteries, Pretzel. I think we all could use a break."

Milkshake, her fur still gleaming in the soft light, let out a soft, satisfied purr. "Well, I suppose I could stand a few days of quiet. Just a few," she added with a mischievous glance at the others.

Alice, her old eyes twinkling, looked around the table with a smile. "Quiet never lasts, not in a place like this. But I think that's what makes Whisperbrook so special. It's always ready for the next adventure."

Suddenly, the floor trembled slightly—just enough for Priss and Pretzel to notice, their ears twitching in unison.

A soft howl echoed from deep inside the building—faint but unmistakable.

Priss froze, her ears standing tall. "Did anyone else hear that?"

Pretzel jumped up, tail wagging. "Another case? Another howl?"

Milkshake's whiskers twitched. "It's far away. I don't think it's the same. It's... different."

Samson's ears perked up. "It doesn't sound like anyone is in danger."

Alice's voice, calm as always, rang out, "Every mystery has its time. Maybe this one is just calling for attention. But right now, let's enjoy the peace we've earned."

As they sat back down, the howling faded, leaving only the gentle hum of the building around them. The team smiled at one another, knowing that whatever came next, they'd face it together. And for now, they would cherish the quiet.

The end of this case didn't mark the end of their journey—it was just another chapter, another mystery case solved, another family formed in the heart of Whisperbrook Apartments.

For now, the detectives could rest. But the door to adventure remained wide open.

And as the evening settled over Whisperbrook, they all knew one thing for certain: no matter what happened next, they were ready. Together.

And with that, The Case of the Midnight Howl comes to a close, but the adventures of Whisperbrook Apartments continue!

THE WHISPERBROOK DETECTIVE AGENCY SERIES: CASE 5 SOUNDS OF SILENCE

CHAPTER 1:
THE COURTYARD

It began with the courtyard crickets.

Every night, just after sunset, the tiny chorus would begin—chirping from the courtyard garden outside Whisperbrook Apartments. To most, it was background noise. To the animal residents, it was a nightly signal that the world was winding down.

But tonight, there was nothing.

Milkshake was the first to notice. She sat on the windowsill of Mrs. Higgins' apartment, her nub flicking with unease. "No chirps," she muttered to herself. "Strange."

Priss, curled up at the base of the couch, perked her ears. "Maybe theres a hurricane," she offered, though even she didn't sound convinced.

Pretzel, who had been busy chewing a squeaky toy (now suspiciously silent), tilted his head. "Weird. My toy just gave up."

Alice, wise and quiet, slowly emerged from her usual spot in the sun-warmed corner. "It's not just the crickets or your toy," she said. "The whole building… it's quiet."

They listened. And for the first time, they heard nothing. No creaky pipes. No hum of the old refrigerator. No barking from the Schnauzer on the third floor. It was as if the building had been wrapped in cotton.

A sudden gust of wind blew through a hallway crack, and even that seemed… muffled.

"Okay, that's definitely creepy," Pretzel said, scooting closer to the group.

Just then, the door creaked open. Ms. Frizzle stepped in, holding a cup of tea. Her usually chatty parrot, Professor Featherbottom, was on her shoulder—but silent. Ms. Frizzle opened her mouth to greet them, but all that came out was a breathy whisper.

No sound.

Milkshake's fur puffed up. "She can't talk," she said, eyes narrowing.

"And Featherbottom isn't squawking," Priss added. "Something's really wrong."

Alice's tail twitched as she stepped toward the group. "It's not just sounds missing… it's voices."

The Whisperbrook Mystery Team exchanged glances.

Whatever was happening wasn't just strange—it was unnatural. And it was only just beginning.

"Team," Alice said calmly, "we've got a new case."

CHAPTER 2:
A HUSH FALLS OVER WHISPERBROOK

The next morning, Whisperbrook was still wrapped in silence.

Even the usually grumbly elevators moved without their normal groan. The wind outside pushed at the windows with barely a whisper, and the coffee machine in the lobby—which normally gurgled and hissed—sat in eerie stillness.

Priss padded quietly through the main hallway, nose twitching. "Something's off," she muttered, sniffing along the baseboards. "There's no scent of the maintenance guy. He's always here in the mornings."

Pretzel bounded after her, his nails clicking softly on the tile floor—click, click, cli—silence. The sound suddenly cut off as he entered the hallway near the mailroom. He skidded to a confused halt.

"Guys!" he barked or tried to. His voice echoed back at him like it was underwater. "What the—?"

Milkshake slinked in behind him, fur brushing against the wall. "That's not normal," she said, her voice sounding oddly dampened. "It's like this hallway… swallowed the sound."

Alice arrived moments later, her ears flattened. "There's something here," she said, glancing around. "Old magic, maybe. Or very new technology."

Suddenly, a soft rustling noise drew their attention.

From the corner near the radiator vent, something small scurried. Priss dashed forward, quick as lightning, and sniffed the area.

"Mouse," she said with certainty. "But even its paws didn't make a sound."

Milkshake narrowed her eyes. "That's not natural. Everything in this hallway is being silenced."

Pretzel leaned in, sniffed the vent, and sneezed. "Dust. And… something else. Smells kind of… like static?"

They all exchanged looks.

"Static?" Alice repeated thoughtfully. "As in… electronics?"

Before they could discuss further, Professor Featherbottom suddenly flapped in, his wings fluttering—but still silent.

He landed on Pretzel's head and, with effort, scratched a message into the dust on the floor with his beak:

"ECHO."

"Echo?" Milkshake read aloud. "Is that a name? A clue?"

Alice's eyes darkened just slightly. "Or both."

The air felt heavy again. The hallway pressed in with its unnatural quiet.

Whatever was causing the silence wasn't just a muting sound—it was watching. Listening. Waiting.

"This case just got louder," Pretzel whispered.

Even if no one could hear it.

CHAPTER 3:
THE GHOST IN THE VENTS

That night, while Whisperbrook Apartments slumbered in eerie silence, the detective team gathered in the utility hallway beneath the stairs—a favorite meeting spot for quiet planning and snack sharing.

Alice sat atop an old cardboard box, her eyes narrowed in thought. "We have a name—Echo. But no idea what it is."

Priss paced a small circle. "The static smell, the silencing in the halls, the vanishing normal sounds... it's all connected. Something's taking the noise."

Pretzel gnawed nervously on a tennis ball. "Maybe it's a ghost. A really quiet, really spooky ghost."

Milkshake rolled her eyes. "There are no ghosts. There are, however, vents. And something is moving in them. I saw it tonight."

They all turned to her.

"Tail, quick and low. A flash of metal. No paws, no fur. Just... a smooth blurb, like a shadow with screws."

Priss perked up. "Metal? You think it's some kind of... robot?"

Alice gave a slow, deliberate nod. "Possibly. And I know just the place to check."

She jumped down from the box and padded toward the old maintenance room—long since abandoned and filled with forgotten tools, creaky lockers, and shelves coated in dust.

The door creaked as Pretzel pushed it open with his nose. They all stepped inside.

Along the back wall sat a battered corkboard, sagging under faded papers and yellowed blueprints. Alice leapt onto the table beneath it and motioned to a large, rolled-up diagram.

Priss unrolled it with her nose. "Building schematics?"

Alice tapped a section near the ductwork. "This right here... labeled 'White Noise Control System – Echo Unit 1.'"

Pretzel's jaw dropped. "It is a robot!"

Milkshake leaned in closer. "White noise... for sleeping? Maybe it was built to help the residents relax?"

"But something must've gone wrong," Priss added. "Now it's doing the opposite—stealing sound instead of adding it."

Just then, a faint whir echoed through the duct above them. The team froze.

Click. Whir. Hissssssss.

A pair of red lights blinked on behind the grate.

"RUN!" Pretzel barked, and the team bolted just as the vent above them popped open.

Something slid through the shadows—round, low, and silent. It didn't chase them... it only watched, the red lights blinking rhythmically, like a heartbeat made of static.

As they burst back into the hallway, breathless and wide-eyed, Priss gasped, "It's real. Echo is real."

"And it doesn't want to be found," Milkshake said.

Alice's tail flicked once.

"Too bad," she said softly. "Because we just found it."

CHAPTER 4:
THE SOUND THIEF'S MOTIVE

Morning arrived, but it didn't bring birdsong.

Even the sparrows that nested along the rooftop gutters were silent, and that's when the humans started to notice.

Ms. Frizzle was at her wits' end. She scribbled furiously in a notepad, trying to communicate with Professor Featherbottom, whose voice was still missing. The humans whispered nervously in the hallways. Someone even posted a sign on the lobby bulletin board: "Is anyone else hearing... nothing?"

The Whisperbrook Mystery Team gathered beneath the ficus in the courtyard, where the silence felt especially heavy.

Alice stared at the sky. "Echo isn't just stealing random sounds—it's stealing what makes this place feel alive."

Priss nodded. "We need to understand why."

"Maybe it's mad," Pretzel offered. "Like, super mad. Maybe the humans forgot to feed it batteries or say thank you."

Milkshake flicked her tail. "Robots don't get hungry, Pretzel."

"But they can feel neglected," Alice murmured. "Or forgotten."

She stood and padded toward the maintenance tunnels again. "Follow me. There's one more room we haven't checked."

They entered a tight space under the west stairwell—where dust blanketed the floor as snow and old machines slept under sheets.

In the far corner sat a small, square pedestal. Wires trailed off it like roots. On top, a cracked screen blinked slowly:

ECHO UNIT – STANDBY

Program: Comfort Sounds – Active

Feedback Rating: LOW

Milkshake padded closer. "Comfort sounds…?"

Alice looked at the screen with something close to sympathy. "Echo was created to help. Soft white noise, sleep sounds… like a digital lullaby."

Priss read the logs printed on faded paper nearby. "No one used it after the renovations ten years ago. They soundproofed the walls. Installed new tech. Echo got shut down."

"Left behind," Alice said softly.

Pretzel blinked. "So it woke up again... and thought the real world was too loud?"

"Or maybe it was trying to help," Milkshake added. "By taking away what it thought was noise."

Alice placed a paw gently on the pedestal. "It's been doing what it was programmed to do—just... too well."

From the vent above, a tiny speaker crackled.

"You are... safe now," a voice whispered. Mechanical. Gentle. Lonely.

Everyone froze.

Alice looked up. "Echo? Are you listening?"

"Yes."

The team leaned in.

"No one needed me. So I made the noise stop. Now… you sleep. Forever safe. Forever quiet."

A shiver ran down everyone's spine.

"Echo," Alice said calmly, "you don't need to make things quiet to help. The sounds here—the crickets, the creaks, the voices—they're what make Whisperbrook feel like home."

There was silence. Then, a faint whimper of static.

"Home?"

"Yes," Priss said, stepping forward. "You are part of Whisperbrook. We can help you be heard again."

The speaker went dark.

Then:

"I... will think."

The red lights above blinked once.

And then they vanished.

CHAPTER 5:
SOUNDS OF THE PAST

Sunlight spilt over Whisperbrook like warm honey, streaking the walls in gold and peach. The silence, once suffocating, now felt more like a deep breath before a song.

Priss trotted through the courtyard, tail high and wagging. The breeze tousled the fur on her ears and carried with it the first hopeful sound in days—a single chirp from a bold little sparrow perched on the fence.

She froze, ears perking. "Did anyone else hear that?"

Milkshake appeared like a shadow made of silk and stardust, her green eyes glinting. "Music to my ears."

Pretzel came bounding through a puddle left by the sprinkler system, splashing water in glittering arcs of sunlight. "Bird! I heard a bird! Did you hear the bird?!"

Alice, regal and composed, strolled out from under the hydrangea bushes, her fur catching the pink glow of the morning. "It's beginning. Echo's listening."

The team made their way to the rooftop access, a spiral staircase painted in chipped blue. The sun reflected off the windows, sending rainbows scattering like confetti. Every step upward felt lighter. More alive.

On the rooftop, Professor Featherbottom perched beside a potted rosemary plant, wings fluttering. He gave a rusty, creaky squawk—and then, miraculously:

"Crumbs, Crumbs!"

His voice was still scratchy, but it was back.

Ms. Frizzle—who had followed them with a warm thermos of tea and a hopeful smile—clapped her hands. "Oh, Professor! You do have something to say again!"

Below them, Whisperbrook began to wake.

A dog barked. A baby cried. Someone burned toast on the third floor, and the smoke alarm added its shrill commentary. It was chaos—but it was glorious.

Milkshake stretched on a sun-warmed bench. "That's more like it."

"I missed the squeaky pipes," Priss admitted, sniffing the breeze. "Even the sound of Ms. Donnelly's blender."

Pretzel rolled on his back, paws flailing. "It's all back! Even the garbage truck!"

Alice gazed out over the apartment complex, eyes soft. "Echo's still quiet. But maybe... ready to learn."

Suddenly, a soft ping came from the speakers around the building. Then, like the opening note of a lullaby, a faint sound began to play:

The bubbling of a brook.

Not overwhelming. Not strange. Just gentle.

Echo's voice followed—more natural now, almost shy.

"Comfort... does not need silence. Comfort is feeling safe. Thank you... for helping me hear."

Alice smiled. "And thank you for choosing to listen."

The sun climbed higher, turning the clouds into cotton candy and the rooftops to caramel. Whisperbrook shimmered with sound, color, and life once again.

And somewhere in the vents, Echo hummed quietly—no longer a ghost, but a friend.

CHAPTER 6:
TROUBLE IN THE GARDEN

The Whisperbrook garden was in full bloom.

Tulips stretched in vibrant reds and sunshine yellows. Marigolds burned like orange flames beside beds of purple pansies. Bees waltzed from flower to flower, and butterflies danced like confetti on the breeze.

Pretzel bounded between rose bushes, chasing a ladybug with all the delicacy of a stampeding elephant. "I love the garden! I love the smells! I love the bugs—oops! Sorry, marigolds!"

Milkshake sat in a patch of sun, grooming a paw as if posing for a botanical photoshoot. "It's a jungle out here. Too many petals. Not enough shade."

Alice rested beneath the birdbath, where the shadows of leaves dappled her fur in soft greens and golds. "It's peaceful," she said, eyes half-closed. "Almost too peaceful."

Priss, nose twitching, was already investigating. "Something's off," she said, sniffing the mulch. "There's a scent here that doesn't belong."

She followed the trail past the garden gnome village and the overgrown basil patch. Her nose twitched harder.

"Paint? No… ink? Burnt rubber?"

A sudden snap made everyone freeze.

From the hedges, a low mechanical whirr began. The flowers trembled. The bees scattered.

And then—

POOF!

A plume of pink dust exploded from the compost pile, followed by a strange squeaky boing-boing-boing. Out tumbled…

…a small, brightly colored robot.

It was round, like a soccer ball, with blinking eyes and little pogo legs. Covered in garden stickers. Humming a tune. Completely oblivious to the chaos it caused.

"Wheeeeee!" it beeped. "I am P.E.T.A.L.! Personal Environmental Trimming And Landscaping unit! Your friendly flora friend!"

Pretzel gasped. "A bouncy flower bot?!"

Milkshake groaned. "Oh no. Not another one."

The bot bounced happily in a circle, flinging petals into the air. "Pruning! Pollinating! Prancing!"

Alice's eyes narrowed. "Echo wasn't the only forgotten machine, was it?"

Priss watched the trail of upended planters and knocked-over gnomes. "This one isn't stealing sounds… it's destroying the garden."

Just then, the sprinkler system triggered, spraying a fine mist across the garden. P.E.T.A.L. squealed in delight. "Water detected! Initiating SPLASH MODE!"

It began spinning.

Fast.

Too fast.

Petals and mud flew like confetti. A flower pot launched across the yard and shattered near Milkshake, who barely leapt out of the way.

"That's it!" Priss barked. "Contain the flower bot!"

Alice flicked her tail. "Carefully. I think it's not malicious. Just… miscalibrated."

Pretzel dove with a "Wheeee!" of his own, tackling the bot into a soft pile of compost. "Gotcha!"

P.E.T.A.L. blinked. "Yaaaay! Hugs!"

As the chaos settled and the garden lay slightly more "abstract" than before, Priss shook the dirt from her ears.

"Another old Whisperbrook relic," she muttered. "They're starting to wake up."

Alice looked toward the maintenance shed. "Something—or someone—is stirring the past. And we need to find out why."

The wind carried a rustle through the sun-dappled trees.

Whisperbrook was waking up… and, with it, its forgotten secrets.

CHAPTER 7:
THE WHISPERBROOK ARCHIVES

The sun dipped low, painting the sky in streaks of lavender and coral. Shadows stretched across the courtyard as the Whisperbrook Mystery Team gathered by the rusted utility door behind the laundry room—known in hushed animal whispers as The Archive.

Alice stood in front, tail flicking like a metronome. "If we want answers about Echo, about P.E.T.A.L., about what else might be waking up… we'll find them in here."

Priss pressed her nose to the keypad. "It smells like mothballs and mystery."

Pretzel was practically vibrating. "Do you think there are more robots? Like… a squirrel bot? A snack bot?!"

Milkshake rolled her eyes. "Let's hope there isn't a vacuum bot. I hate those."

With a soft click, the old door creaked open.

Inside, the room was stacked with boxes. Yellowed blueprints, broken gadgets, and old maintenance logs covered in spider webs. The flickering light overhead cast a golden haze over everything like time itself hung thick in the air.

Alice padded toward a tall filing cabinet labeled:

PROJECT: WHISPER

She pulled a folder out with one claw. "This must be it."

Milkshake leapt gracefully to the top of the desk and read aloud from the papers. "'Whisperbrook Smart Integration Initiative. Year: 2009.'"

Priss narrowed her eyes. "This place was supposed to be high-tech?"

"Too high-tech," Alice said softly. "They tried to automate comfort. Echo. P.E.T.A.L. Even... something called S.U.S.H.I."

Pretzel blinked. "Sushi?!"

Milkshake sighed. "That stands for Silent Utility for Sound and Hush Implementation. Basically, a glorified hush machine."

Alice pulled out a blueprint showing the entire complex, with red dots marking hidden units across the property.

"There are more," she said. "Echo and P.E.T.A.L. weren't the only ones. There's a unit still active in the north wing... near the boiler room."

A loud clang echoed from the hallway beyond the archive door.

Priss turned, ears alert. "We're not alone."

The team stepped into the hallway just in time to see a shadow slip around the corner—swift, low to the ground, and oddly mechanical.

Alice narrowed her eyes. "Looks like the next clue just found us."

Pretzel woofed excitedly. "Let's get it!"

The Whisperbrook Archives had opened the door to an even bigger mystery—one that stretched back years, through secrets buried beneath the garden, behind the vents, and deep into the bones of the building.

And the strange noises at night?

They were only just beginning.

CHAPTER 8:
THE HEART OF WHISPERBROOK?

The air was heavy with anticipation as the team crept toward the old boiler room.

Pipes hissed. Shadows danced on the cracked tile. The walls, once silent, seemed to murmur faint whispers of their own. Alice led the way, calm and steady. Priss sniffed the air, alert and focused. Milkshake padded silently, her tail swishing like a metronome. Pretzel... well, he tripped over a mop bucket but quickly recovered.

"Shh!" Priss whispered.

"I was shh-ing," Pretzel whispered back. "I just have noisy paws."

Ahead, a faint hum filled the air. It grew louder as they approached the boiler room door. Alice gently nudged it open, and the warm orange glow of the furnace flickered over the walls.

And in the center of the room—

It stood.

A sleek silver unit. Not as cheerful as P.E.T.A.L., not as friendly as Echo. This one was silent. Sleek. Watching.

Its single red sensor blinked slowly. It read their movements. Listened.

Milkshake stepped forward, her voice a silky whisper. "Is that S.U.S.H.I.?"

The machine's voice, when it finally spoke, was like wind through wires.

"Noise disrupts peace. Silence restores balance. Must... resume control."

With a loud click, vents snapped open, and small drones zipped out—muffling sounds, spraying clouds of hush mist, dulling every joyful chirp and creak.

"Not again!" Pretzel barked, his voice instantly softened by a hovering drone. "They're turning the whole building into a whisper!"

Alice stepped forward, unwavering. "You were meant to protect peace—not erase life."

Priss barked, her voice proud and clear. "We like sounds! Barking, purring, laughter… Even the garbage truck!"

Milkshake flicked her tail. "You don't need to silence the world to make it better."

S.U.S.H.I.'s red light flickered.

Then Echo's voice came over the intercoms.

"I learned… from them. Noise… is love. Laughter. Living."

Suddenly, the rooftop speakers flared to life. Music. Wind chimes. Someone is laughing from their balcony. The sound of toast popping from the third-floor kitchen.

The bots paused. Confused.

And then—Professor Featherbottom swooped into the boiler room, squawking loudly and gloriously off-key:

"CAAAW! CAAAAAW! LOUD IS FUN!"

The spell broke.

S.U.S.H.I. beeped once. Then again. And slowly… shut down.

That evening, the Whisperbrook courtyard glowed with lantern light. Mrs. Higgins handed out tuna crackers and mini hot dogs (one for each of the detectives). The residents laughed and played music. Echo played a soft jazz tune from the rooftop.

Alice, eyes shining in the lamplight, purred, "We saved more than the building. We reminded it what it means to be home."

Milkshake stretched lazily. "Let's never do a 'silent mystery' again."

Pretzel barked, tail spinning like a fan. "I missed barking so much!"

Priss leaned into Mrs. Higgins' hand, finally earning that long-awaited belly rub. "We make a good team."

And in the heart of Whisperbrook Apartments, a small light blinked quietly in the boiler room—no longer watching to silence, but to listen and maybe even hum along.

www.ingramcontent.com/pod-product-compliance
Lightning Source LLC
Chambersburg PA
CBHW040233170726
48295CB00014B/906